MEG'S EGGS

for Katie

MEG'S EGGS

by Helen Nicoll
and Jan Pieńkowski

PUFFIN BOOKS

She
put
in

lizards, newts, 2 green frogs

supper

any

without

to bed

went

and

In the
middle
of the
night Meg
heard

Meg's egg was hatching

Meg took Diplodocus to

the pond

Diplodocus was very happy

Mog
took
Stegosaurus
into
the
garden

Owl
was
watching
the
last
egg

Out
jumped
Tyrannosaurus,
the
most
ferocious
of
all
the
dinosaurs

SNAP

They
were

very
frightened

Tyrannosaurus wanted to eat them all

Meg flew home and tried
to make a good spell

Bacon and eggs
Jump over their legs
Those 3 big lumps
Will be 3 little bumps

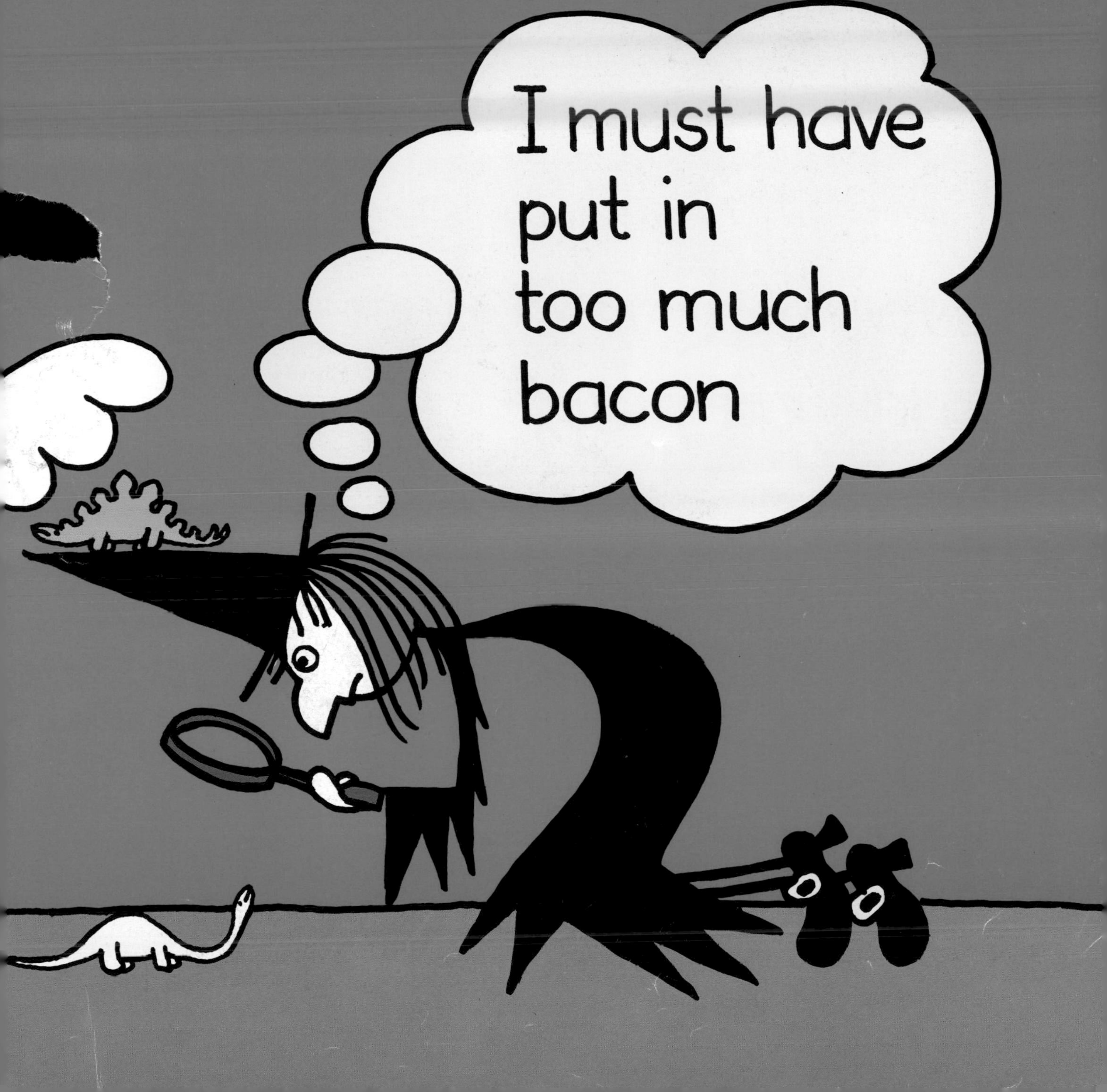
I must have put in too much bacon

Goodbye!